D1297941

EVERYDAY MINDFULNESS
Sleep Easy

Published in North America by Free Spirit Publishing Inc., Minneapolis, Minnesota, 2018

North American rights reserved under International and Pan-American Copyright Conventions. Unless otherwise noted, no part of this book may be reproduced, stored in a retrieval system, or transmitted in any form or by any means, electronic, mechanical, photocopying, or otherwise, without express written permission of the publisher, except for brief quotations or critical reviews. For more information, go to www.freespirit.com/permissions.

Free Spirit, Free Spirit Publishing, and associated logos are trademarks and/or registered trademarks of Free Spirit Publishing Inc. A complete listing of our logos and trademarks is available at www.freespirit.com.

Library of Congress Cataloging-in-Publication Data
Names: Christelis, Paul, author. | Paganelli, Elisa, 1985– illustrator.
Title: Sleep easy : a mindfulness guide to getting a good night's sleep / written by Paul Christelis ; illustrated by Elisa Paganelli.
Description: Minneapolis, Minnesota : Free Spirit Publishing, 2018. | Series: Everyday mindfulness | Audience: Age 5–9.
Identifiers: LCCN 2017060599 | ISBN 9781631983344 (hardcover) | ISBN 1631983342 (hardcover)
Subjects: LCSH: Sleep—Juvenile literature.
Classification: LCC RA786 .C487 2018 | DDC 613.7/94—dc23 LC record available at https://lccn.loc.gov/2017060599

Free Spirit Publishing does not have control over or assume responsibility for author or third-party websites and their content.

Reading Level Grade 2; Interest Level Ages 5–9; Fountas & Pinnell Guided Reading Level L

10 9 8 7 6 5 4 3 2 1
Printed in China
H13660518

Free Spirit Publishing Inc.
6325 Sandburg Road, Suite 100
Minneapolis, MN 55427-3674
(612) 338-2068
help4kids@freespirit.com
www.freespirit.com

First published in 2018 by Franklin Watts, a division of Hachette Children's Books • London, UK, and Sydney, Australia

Copyright © The Watts Publishing Group, 2018

The rights of Paul Christelis to be identified as the author and Elisa Paganelli as the illustrator of this Work have been asserted in accordance with the Copyright, Designs and Patents Act, 1988.

Managing editor: Victoria Brooker
Creative design: Lisa Peacock

Free Spirit offers competitive pricing.
Contact edsales@freespirit.com for pricing information on multiple quantity purchases.

Sleep Easy

A MINDFULNESS GUIDE TO GETTING A GOOD NIGHT'S SLEEP

Written by
Paul Christelis

Illustrated by
Elisa Paganelli

free spirit
PUBLISHING®

WHAT IS MINDFULNESS?

Mindfulness is a way of paying attention to our present-moment experience with an attitude of kindness and curiosity. Most of the time, our attention is distracted—often by thoughts about the past or future—and this can make us feel jumpy, worried, unhappy, and confused. By gently moving our focus from our busy minds into the present moment (for example, by noticing how our bodies are feeling), we begin to let go of distraction and learn to tap into an ever-present supply of well-being and ease that resides in each moment. Mindfulness can also help us improve concentration, calm difficult emotions, and even boost our immune systems.

This book shows how mindfulness can support children as they settle down to sleep. It can be read interactively, allowing readers to pause at various points to turn their attention to what they are noticing.

Watch for the `[PAUSE BUTTON]` in the text. It suggests opportunities to encourage readers to be curious about what's going on for them—in their minds, their bodies, and their breathing. You can do this in the form of an invitation:

"Let's take a break from the story and see what we can notice right now. It's a bit like inviting your attention to move away from the story and into your mind, body, or breath. Close your eyes and see what you can feel . . ."

Invite children to verbally share what they are noticing, reminding them that there are no right or wrong responses. There is simply their personal experience. You can share your experience too!

Each time this `[PAUSE BUTTON]` is used, mindfulness is deepened. Research shows that, on a neurological level, the brain actually changes shape when consistent mindfulness is cultivated over time. Our brains are "rewired," replacing patterns that support distraction with new circuits that help foster concentration and calm.

So try not to rush this pause. Really allow enough time for children to tune into their experience. It doesn't matter if what they notice feels pleasant or unpleasant. What's important is to pay attention to it with a friendly attitude. (It's also perfectly fine not to feel anything, and to be curious about this: What is the feeling of "nothing"?) This will introduce children to a way of being in the world that promotes health and happiness.

Have you ever had a hard time trying to get to sleep?
Sometimes our busy minds can keep us awake
with thoughts and worries and jumbles and
mumbles and . . . well, anything you can think of!

Twins Billy and Betty sometimes have this problem.
When Billy gets into bed, his head can be full
of wondering thoughts.

"I wonder if I'll be picked for the soccer team."

"I wonder what presents I'll get for my birthday."

His sister, Betty, is kept awake by a Worry Truck driving around in her head.

"Mom, help! We're wide awake! Will we **ever** fall asleep?"

Luckily, Mom knows a thing or two about a good night's sleep.
"Come on kids, let's get you back to bed," she says. "I'll show you
an easy-peasy way to drift off to dreamland."

The twins climb back into their beds, **curious** about how they'll be able to settle their racing minds.

"Close your eyes and lie in a comfy position," says Mom. "If you feel comfortable, your whole body will start to relax."

Betty lies on her back.
Billy lies on his side.

PAUSE BUTTON

Do you have a favorite bedtime posture? On your tummy, maybe? Or stretched out like a cat in the sun?

Next Mom says, "Notice the feeling of your skin against the sheets. What about your fingers and toes? Do they tingle? Or maybe they feel warm or cold."

Betty's legs are a little achy from so much skipping and running. She hadn't **noticed** that until now.

Billy notices how warm he feels. And his skin
is still tingling from his bubble bath!

PAUSE BUTTON

There is so much to
notice in your body if you
decide to pay attention to
it. Right now, what do
you notice?

Before long, the wonders and worries and jumbles and mumbles return.

"Don't worry if your minds get busy again," Mom says. "See if you can notice your thoughts as they come and go. Watching thoughts is a bit like watching clouds in the sky: They seem to appear from nowhere, sail past, and then disappear."

The children watch their thoughts coming and going.

Thoughts can be words, pictures, voices, memories, plans . . .
anything that makes the mind cloudy.

"Just as you can't stop clouds from forming in the sky, you can't **stop** thoughts from appearing in your mind," Mom explains.

"So allow them to come and go. You can even **smile** at your thoughts. Yes, even the not-so-nice ones! After all, they are only thoughts."

PAUSE BUTTON

Right now, what thoughts do you notice? Close your eyes and see which ones float by. Remember: They are just thoughts!

"Now that you've noticed your busy minds," says Mom, "there's something else you need to find."

Billy wonders what this could be. And where is it? Under the bed?

Mom laughs. "No, silly Billy! What you need to find is much closer to you than that!"

"Is it under the pillow?" asks Betty.

"It's right under your nose," says Mom. "And it's also IN your nose! You can't see it, but you can feel it."

Betty and Billy suddenly get the answer.
"It's our **breath!**" they say.

👆 ▸ PAUSE BUTTON

Whatever you do and wherever you go,
your breath is always with you. And if you
move your attention from your busy mind
and into your breath, you will make a very
interesting discovery. Billy and Betty are
about to find out what that is . . .

"Imagine you are doctors inspecting your breath," says Mom.

"Can you **feel** your breath moving in your belly?"

"Is it smooth like silk or wobbly like jelly?
Maybe it's long, or perhaps it's short.
Maybe it feels warm or cool."

Betty notices that her breath feels cool and smooth, like a
chocolate milkshake sliding down her throat into her belly.

At first, Billy can't easily feel his breathing. So he puts his hands on his belly. Now he can feel his breath rising and falling, like a balloon inflating and deflating.

 **PAUSE BUTTON**

How does your breath feel? Notice it moving in your nose, or in your chest or belly.

After a few moments of paying **attention** to their breathing, the children make a very interesting discovery—there are no busy thoughts anymore! No worries, or jumbles, or mumbles. There is only peace and quiet . . . and the gentle feeling of breathing.

All this peace and quiet is making them sleepy.
Mom tucks them in and turns down the light.
"Before I leave, I have one last tip for getting
the best night's sleep," she says.
"What's that?" the children ask drowsily.

"Once you've made friends with your breath,
try to remember three nice things that happened
to you in the day. They can be big or small."

Betty remembers the taste of the fruity lollipop she had after lunch. She remembers how good it felt when her teacher said "well done" for trying so hard in the spelling test. And playing with her neighbor's puppy—that was nice too!

Billy smiles as he recalls the fun he had banging the drums in music class. It was also exciting to get an invitation to his friend Tom's birthday party. And . . . he can't think of a third thing.

But it doesn't take him long to realize that the third nice thing is happening right now: He is comfy and sleepy in bed, making friends with his breath!

PAUSE BUTTON

Can you recall three nice things that happened to you today? It doesn't matter how small they might be. Remembering to do this every night before bedtime will help relax your body and mind.

NOTES FOR PARENTS AND TEACHERS

Here are a few mindfulness exercises and suggestions to add to children's Mindfulness Toolkits. These are simple, effective, and fun to do!

The Breath Buddy Exercise

Ask each child to choose a small object—such as a small cuddly toy—lie down, and place the object on his or her belly. This object is now a Breath Buddy. The aim of the exercise is to carefully watch the Breath Buddy move as the belly inflates and deflates. Have children see how long their attention can remain on the bobbing object before their mind wanders. When it does wander, bring attention back to the Breath Buddy. If the mind is very busy, the child can also silently count breaths until 10 are completed, and then count another 10, this time counting backward from 10 to 1.

Nuts and Marshmallows

To help the body relax before bedtime, encourage children to let go of any tension they are holding, which is often in the form of muscular tension. You can demonstrate how to do this by having them feel a nut (hard) and comparing this to handling a marshmallow (soft). Then suggest that they use their breathing to gradually change their bodies from nuts into marshmallows. Ask them to imagine breathing out all the tightness, leaving their bodies less "nutty" and more "marshmallowy." If they do this in bed, can they notice their bodies sinking a little deeper into the mattress each time they breathe out?

Another way to let go of tension is to intentionally tighten or clench the body from head to toe. Hold this for a few seconds, then let go and feel the muscles slacken back into a more relaxed state. Do this three or four times, each time noticing all the sensations that accompany the tensing and relaxing.

Talk About Thoughts

Talk to children about the kinds of thoughts they have when they get into bed. Some thoughts are pleasant, some are unpleasant, and some don't feel pleasant or unpleasant. *All* thoughts are okay to have, and everyone has them. Simply making space to identify thoughts in a calm and interested way will help normalize them—especially unpleasant, worrying thoughts.

It can be very helpful for children (and adults!) to understand that they are not their thoughts. If you think a thought often enough, you may start to identify it as being "me"—it can feel like you *are* your thought. But if you look closely you will see that a thought has no substance. You cannot hold a thought in your hand; you cannot see or touch a thought. Clouds are similar: They look white and fluffy from a distance, but if you get closer to them you realize this is just an illusion.

Explore this idea with children. Reassure them that it's okay if worries or other thoughts keep returning. This is normal. A core skill of mindfulness is to keep returning to the sensations of the body and the breath when your attention has slipped back to thoughts. Every time you bring your attention back to the body you are strengthening your "attention muscle."

Practice this together: Move your attention up and down from mind to body. You can notice what thoughts are present (maybe saying them aloud) and then turn your attention to your hands and notice how they are feeling. Then return to your thoughts for a few moments before shifting your focus to another body part, such as your feet, chest, or face. You can "yo-yo" up and down from thoughts to body as many times as you like.

Setting a Bedtime Routine

Talk to children about preparing to go to bed. Do they have a routine, such as brushing teeth, putting on pajamas, and reading (or hearing) a bedtime story? A routine creates a safe and familiar atmosphere that can help our minds settle. It's also good to avoid all digital devices for at least an hour before going to bed because the light from screens can inhibit the natural release of melatonin in the body. Encourage children to take some time to purposefully switch off devices and put them to sleep for the night—a healthy habit for adults to cultivate too!

BOOKS TO SHARE

Acorns to Great Oaks: Meditations for Children by Marie Delanote, illustrated by Jokanies (Findhorn Press, 2017)

Breathe and Be: A Book of Mindfulness Poems by Kate Coombs, illustrated by Anna Emilia Laitinen (Sounds True, 2017)

Breathe Like a Bear: 30 Mindful Moments for Kids to Feel Calm and Focused Anytime, Anywhere by Kira Willey, illustrated by Anni Betts (Rodale Kids, 2017)

I Am Peace: A Book of Mindfulness by Susan Verde, illustrated by Peter H. Reynolds (Abrams Books for Young Readers, 2017)

Sitting Still Like a Frog: Mindfulness Exercises for Kids (and Their Parents) by Eline Snel (Shambhala Publications, 2013)

Visiting Feelings by Lauren Rubenstein, illustrated by Shelly Hehenberger (Magination Press, 2014)

What Does It Mean to Be Present? by Rana DiOrio, illustrated by Eliza Wheeler (Little Pickle Stories, 2010)

A World of Pausabilities: An Exercise in Mindfulness by Frank J. Sileo, illustrated by Jennifer Zivoin (Magination Press, 2017)